# A Royal Easter

By Andrea Posner-Sanchez
Illustrated by Francesco Legramandi and Gabriella Matta

A Random House PICTUREBACK® Book
Random House 🏠 New York

Published in the United States by Random House Children's Books, a division of Random House LLC, a Penguin Random House Company, 1745 Broadway, New York, NY 10019, and in Canada by Random House of Canada Limited, Toronto, in conjunction with Disney Enterprises, Inc. Pictureback, Random House, and the Random House colophon are registered trademarks of Random House LLC.
randomhouse.com/kids
ISBN 978-0-7364-3084-5
Printed in the United States of America
10 9 8 7 6 5 4 3 2

Easter has arrived! Princesses everywhere are enjoying the spring season.

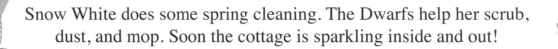

Snow White does some spring cleaning. The Dwarfs help her scrub, dust, and mop. Soon the cottage is sparkling inside and out!

Belle is planting flowers in the Beast's garden.

Mrs. Potts pitches in and gives the flowers a drink.

Rapunzel paints Easter decorations on the tower walls.

Pascal blends in nicely with the springtime colors!

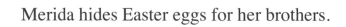

Merida hides Easter eggs for her brothers.

Uh-oh! It looks as though they've already found some chocolates!

Scuttle has an Easter surprise for Ariel from the human world.

The little mermaid isn't sure what it is, but she loves it!

Cinderella makes Easter bonnets for all her friends.

Now they are ready for a parade!

Tiana bakes a sweet Easter treat!

© Disney

© Disney

© Disney

© Disney•Pixar

© Disney

© Disney

© Disney

© Disney

© Disney

© Disney